# The *Witch* Goes to School

## by NORMAN BRIDWELL

### Hello Reader! — Level 3

## SCHOLASTIC INC.

New York   Toronto   London   Auckland   Sydney

Our next-door neighbor is a
good friend of ours. She also
happens to be a witch.

# A NOTE TO PARENTS

### Reading Aloud with Your Child

*Research shows that reading books aloud is the single most valuable support parents can provide in helping children learn to read.*

- Be a ham! The more enthusiasm you display, the more your child will enjoy the book.
- Run your finger underneath the words as you read to signal that the print carries the story.
- Leave time for examining the illustrations more closely; encourage your child to find things in the pictures.
- Invite your youngster to join in whenever there's a repeated phrase in the text.
- Link up events in the book with similar events in your child's life.
- If your child asks a question, stop and answer it. The book can be a means to learning more about your child's thoughts.

### Listening to Your Child Read Aloud

*The support of your attention and praise is absolutely crucial to your child's continuing efforts to learn to read.*

- If your child is learning to read and asks for a word, give it immediately so that the meaning of the story is not interrupted. DO NOT ask your child to sound out the word.
- On the other hand, if your child initiates the act of sounding out, don't intervene.
- If your child is reading along and makes what is called a miscue, listen for the sense of the miscue. If the word "road" is substituted for the word "street," for instance, no meaning is lost. Don't stop the reading for a correction.
- If the miscue makes no sense (for example, "horse" for "house"), ask your child to reread the sentence because you're not sure you understand what's just been read.
- Above all else, enjoy your child's growing command of print and make sure you give lots of praise. *You are your child's first teacher—and the most important one. Praise from you is critical for further risk-taking and learning.*

—Priscilla Lynch
Ph.D., New York University
Educational Consultant

To Mary Gentle
—N.B.

No part of this publication may be reproduced in whole or in part, or stored in a retrieval system, or transmitted in any form or by any means, electronic, mechanical, photocopying, recording, or otherwise, without written permission of the publisher. For information regarding permission, write to Scholastic Inc., 730 Broadway, New York, NY 10003.

Library of Congress Cataloging-in-Publication Data

Bridwell, Norman.
    The witch goes to school / by Norman Bridwell.
      p.    cm. — (Hello reader)
    Summary: A normal day at school becomes special when the Witch comes for a visit and uses her magic.
    ISBN 0-590-45831-0
    [1. Witches—Fiction.  2. Magic—Fiction.  3. Schools—Fiction.]
I. Title.  II. Series.
PZ7.B7633Wh  1992
[E]—dc20
                                    92-12091
                                        CIP
                                        AC

12  11  10  9  8                                   4  5  6  7/9

First Scholastic printing, August 1992

One day we were late for school.
Our witch said she would
get us there on time.

And she did.

We got to our room just before
the bell rang. Our teacher was surprised.

She invited the witch to stay for a visit.
It was show-and-tell time. Kevin showed us
his tooth that came out that morning.

I said I had lost one of my teeth,
but I forgot to bring it to school.
The witch just waved her hands. . . .

The tooth fairy flew in.
She had my tooth.

She said I could have a quarter
if I let her keep it, so I did.
She gave Kevin a quarter for his tooth, too.

The tooth fairy was the hit
of show-and-tell time.
After she left, we did silent reading.
That is always fun.

I was sure that I saw real dinosaurs come out of my brother's book. I thought our witch was working her magic.

She said she wasn't. Books are like that.
Sometimes they seem real.

At recess, we all ran outside.
I wanted to get to the slide first.
The slide is my favorite.

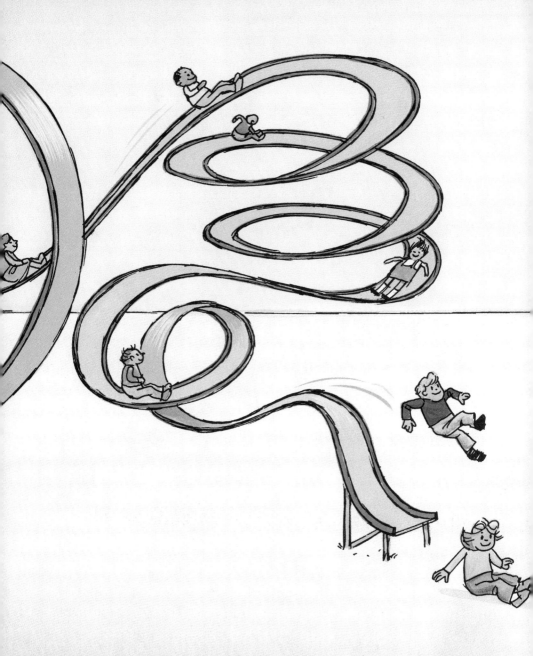

The witch made the slide more fun than
it had ever been before.

And she turned the jungle gym
into a real jungle.

Then there was some trouble.
A big kid wouldn't let a little
kid come down from the seesaw.

Our witch doesn't like that kind of teasing.

After recess, we had writing. I couldn't think of anything good to write about.

I asked the witch to help me.
She wouldn't.
She said that wouldn't be fair.

I tried a little harder and I wrote
a story I was really proud of.

It was about the day
our witch came to school!

We went to the cafeteria for lunch.

That big kid was there. He grabbed my brother's peanut butter sandwich.

Then the sandwich grabbed him.
What a mess!

One of the cafeteria ladies gets upset if we don't eat all our food.

The kids were in luck.
Our witch likes leftovers.

She felt a little full. . . .

But she was fine by the time we walked back
to our classroom.

That afternoon, we went on a nature walk.
Our teacher said that we would see some
interesting animals.

She was right. We saw mice, birds, rabbits, and squirrels.

We even found a frog
and a snail.

Then the witch showed us some animals that we had never seen in the woods before.

What an exciting field trip!
The animals took us for rides.

Then we said good-bye
and walked back to school.

Our teacher thanked our witch for making
the day so much fun. Our witch thanked
our teacher for making every day so special.